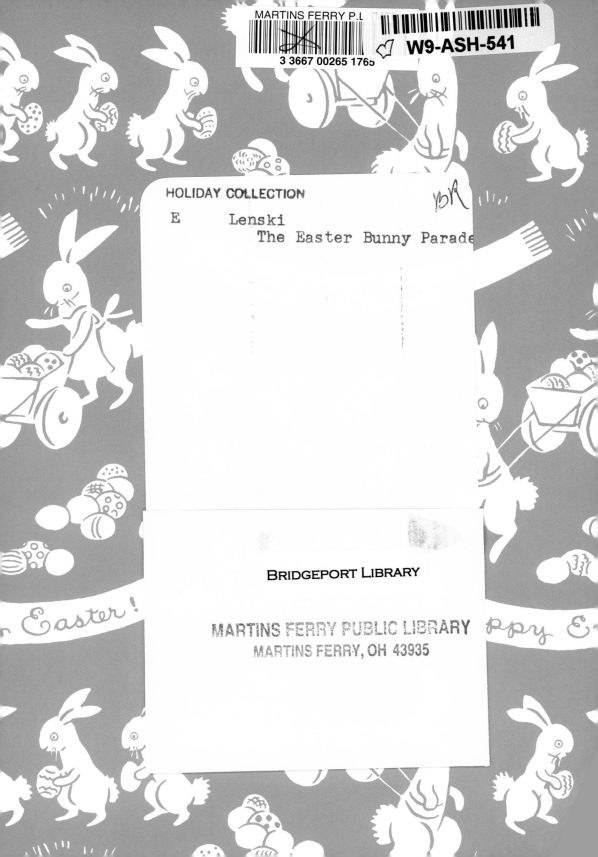

The EASTER RABBIT'S PARADE

Copyright © 1936 by Lois Lenski. Copyright renewed 1964 by the Lois Lenski Covey Foundation.
All rights reserved under International and Pan-American Copyright Conventions. Published in the
United States by Random House Children's Books, a division of Random House, Inc., New York,
and simultaneously in Canada by Random House of Canada Limited, Toronto. Originally published
in slightly different form by Oxford University Press, Inc., in 1936.

www.randomhouse.com/kids

Library of Congress Cataloging-in-Publication Data
Lenski, Lois.
The Easter Rabbit's parade / by Lois Lenski. — 1st Random House ed.
p.   cm.
SUMMARY: Ann Eliza takes very good care of the farmyard animals, so despite the grumbling of
Graybeard the Goat and the bragging of White Rabbit, they work together to make a very nice
Easter for her.
ISBN 0-375-82748-X (trade) — ISBN 0-375-92748-4 (lib. bdg.)
[1. Easter—Fiction. 2. Domestic animals—Fiction. 3. Gratitude—Fiction.] I. Title. PZ7.L54 Eas
2004
[E]—dc21
2003008116

MANUFACTURED IN MALAYSIA   10 9 8 7 6 5 4 3 2 1

First Random House Edition 2004
RANDOM HOUSE and colophon are registered trademarks of Random House, Inc.

The EASTER RABBIT'S PARADE

by LOIS LENSKI

Random House New York

Ann Eliza had a Farmyard with ducks and animals and fowls. Ann Eliza fed and watered them every day. She swept out their coops and cleaned out their troughs. She pumped water and carried it in pails. She shelled corn and sprinkled grain. She pulled carrots and lettuce from the garden. She took very good care of the Farmyard.

Winter was gone and spring was on the way. The grass was green again and all the buds were bursting. It was going to be EASTER! The animals said, "We will make Easter for Ann Eliza."

Little Brown Hen stood up in front and asked, *"What will you give for Ann Eliza?"*

The animals thought for a long time.

At last Little Brown Hen said, "I will give her eggs from my beautiful nest of yellow straw."

Web-foot the Duck said, "I will dive down into the big pond and bring up pretty stones and shells and polish them on my wings."

Mother Sheep said, "I will give my soft warm wool to make her a coverlid."

"But it's *Spring!*" growled Old Graybeard the Goat.

Little Brown Hen asked, "Where will we get a basket for Ann Eliza?"

The animals thought for a long time.

The pigeons said, "We will make a basket from the curly shavings the farmer left in his carpenter shop. We will stick them together with clay from the pond."

The geese said, "We will give our down and fluffy feathers to put in the bottom and make it soft."

The swans said, "We will lay a golden egg to put in the middle."

"Don't believe it!" growled Old Graybeard the Goat.

Little Brown Hen asked, "Who will make music for Ann Eliza?"

The animals thought for a long time.

"I will gobble," said the turkey.

"I will moo," said the cow.

"I will neigh and whinny," said the horse.

"I will grunt," said the pig.

"We will sing," said the birds.

"I will crow under her window," said Red Rooster.

"And you'll wake up everybody," muttered Old Graybeard the Goat.

Little Brown Hen asked, *"Who will get flowers for Ann Eliza?"*

The animals thought and thought for a long time.

The baby chicks said, "We will pick crocuses by the garden gate."

The goslings said, "We will pick violets and primroses in the field."

"Watch out you don't get weeds," growled Old Graybeard the Goat.

Just then, White Rabbit came bouncing in from the Hayfield. He held his head high in the air and wiggled it and sniffed. He was very wet.

"Where have you been, White Rabbit?" asked Web-foot the Duck.

"Oh, I just went for a swim."

"Why, rabbits don't swim!"

"That's very true. Rabbits hate swimming, but I got up my courage and used my tail for a pusher and so I won the race!" He wiggled his nose and sniffed again.

"**W**hat race?" asked Old Graybeard the Goat.

"The Frog and Turtle Race, of course."

"But how did you ever get into *that*?"

"Well, you see, it was this way. As I came along over the bridge, Grandpa Fish called out, 'Everybody in!' and I stumbled over a turtle and was *in*!"

"**Y**ou mean you *fell* in?" asked Web-foot.

"Oh well, call it what you like, *I* don't care. Anyhow, I won FIRST PRIZE! Why don't you ask me what it was?"

"Don't want to know!" growled Old Graybeard the Goat.

"Well, what was it?" asked Web-foot politely.

"A beautiful white lily in a flower pot."

"Ho! Ho! That's a likely
story!" muttered
Old Graybeard the Goat.

"And I'm giving it to Ann Eliza for Easter. So
there!"

White Rabbit sniffed and turned the other way. It
was very plain that White Rabbit and Old Graybeard
the Goat didn't like each other.

White Rabbit looked around and saw that the animals were having a meeting.

"Dear me, dear me, what's all this hullabaloo about?" he asked. The animals looked at each other in silence. White Rabbit always scared them a little.

"Why . . . ," said Little Brown Hen.

"We were just . . . ," hesitated Mother Sheep.

"We thought . . . we thought we would make Easter for Ann Eliza," sputtered Gray Goose.

"EASTER! EASTER! What do farmyard animals know about EASTER, anyway?" White Rabbit tossed his head and sniffed loudly. "Only Rabbits know about Easter. Don't all the children call me Easter Rabbit?"

He threw back his head, cleared his throat, and sang:

"Easter Rabbit, so they call me,
Easter Rabbit fine and gay.
Every spring I bring the children
Easter eggs on Easter Day."

"**Y**es, but I lay the eggs," said Little Brown Hen.

"But you lay just plain eggs. They're not Easter eggs until I color them. What do you know about paint?"

"Nothing," said Little Brown Hen, and hid her face under her wing.

"Very well, then," said White Rabbit with a wave of his arm. "Bring out your eggs while I call my children."

White Rabbit hopped out the gate into the Hayfield. In a moment he came back followed by his wife and children. Mrs. Rabbit carried a pile of mixing bowls. The baby rabbits brought rabbit-hair brushes and paints.

White Rabbit marched at the head of the procession.

"Yes, I'm the Easter Rabbit." He talked to himself, but very loudly. "That's what the children call me. All the children love me and hunt for my eggs. . . ."

"I beg your pardon, *whose* eggs?" asked Little Brown Hen.

"Well, I suppose you do *lay* them. . . ."

"And *who* boils them hard?"

"Oh well, you do that, too, I suppose. Have it your own way. Which reminds me, are they boiled yet?"

"**O**h yes!" said Little Brown Hen. "What do you think I have been doing all the time you've been talking? Ann Eliza's eggs must be all ready to eat. Here they are."

She spread the eggs on the grass.

White Rabbit waved his brush and palette in the air. "Get away, everybody! Get away, everybody! *We* color the eggs."

He began to sing loudly and very gaily:

> *"Easter Rabbit, so they call me,*
> *Easter Rabbit fine and gay.*
> *Every spring I bring the children*
> *Easter eggs on Easter Day."*

"What a song," said Old Graybeard the Goat.

"Make up a better one, then," said White Rabbit.

Mrs. Rabbit scurried about, filled her bowls with hot water from Little Brown Hen's kettle, and set to work. From the pocket in her apron she took an envelope full of pills of different colors and dropped one pill into each bowl. She then set a baby rabbit to stir it with a stick until each bowl was filled with brightly colored dye—red, yellow, blue, green, orange, and purple.

One by one Mrs. Rabbit dropped the eggs into the bowls. The baby rabbits watched the eggs carefully until it was time to take them out. Then Mrs. Rabbit lifted each egg with a spoon and laid it on the grass to dry.

All this time White Rabbit was leaning against a tree, singing his song:

> *"Easter Rabbit, so they call me,*
> *Easter Rabbit fine and gay.*

Hey there, wait a minute!" He jumped up quickly. "I want to paint those eggs!" He bounced over the lawn, took up a paintbrush, and began to paint flowers and dogs and curlicues and pretty pictures on the eggs. Then he gave a big yawn and fell over backward. "That's enough for this time . . . ," he murmured.

In a moment he was fast asleep. Mrs. Rabbit went quietly to work to clean up, and the baby rabbits helped.

Nobody knew how it happened, but just as Mrs. Rabbit was emptying the bowls of dye, one of them slipped. Purple dye was sprinkled far and wide, most of it on White Rabbit's face!

The whole Farmyard saw it and set up a great roar and cackle. Even quiet little Mrs. Rabbit had to hold her sides and laugh.

"Oh, see pretty Freckle Face!" roared Old Graybeard the Goat.

"What's all this? What's all this?" White Rabbit woke up in a hurry. "Why are you all laughing?"

"Freckle Face! Freckle Face! Freckle Face!" called everyone from Mother Sheep down to the tiniest gosling.

White Rabbit crept to the pool, leaned over, and took one look.

"Oh dear, oh dear, and the day before Easter, too. . . ."

Easter morning came at last. The whole world was beautiful. Rain had washed the garden the night before, but at dawn the sun came out warm and bright. It awoke the crocuses along the path and the flowers in the grass. It awoke the animals in the Farmyard and the Hayfield.

Ann Eliza dressed slowly. She looked in the corners of the room, but there were no eggs there. She looked behind the doors and in the closets, but she couldn't find any Easter eggs. She ate her porridge tearfully.

Ann Eliza ran out into the yard. She looked in the grass and under the bushes, but there were no eggs there. She sat down on the grass and hid her face in her hands. "Oh dear," she thought, "I must give the animals their breakfast."

Suddenly she heard a great clucking and bustling and baaing and cackling and chirping, the cooing of doves and pigeons, the singing of birds, the crowing of roosters.

Ann Eliza looked and there came the Easter Parade from the Farmyard, chickens and ducks and roosters and pigeons and sheep and swans and baby chicks and goslings.

They all made a circle around her, and in her lap they put a beautiful Easter basket. It was filled with Easter eggs of red and blue and green and purple, and some of them had dots and curlicues and pretty pictures painted on them.

Around the edge was a row of lovely colored stones and shiny shells. The eggs rested on silvery feathers and fluffy down, and underneath all was a cozy lamb's wool coverlid. Right in the center was an egg of gold.

"*We* made the basket," said the pigeons.

"*We* put the feathers in the bottom," said the geese.

"*I* laid the eggs," said Little Brown Hen.

"You don't say so!" muttered Old Graybeard the Goat.

"*I* found the pretty stones and shells," said Web-foot the Duck.

"*I* laid the egg of gold," said Long Neck the Swan.

"*We* picked the flowers," said the baby chicks and goslings.

"Oh, did you now?" mumbled Old Graybeard the Goat.

Ann Eliza was so happy she could not speak. She had never seen such a beautiful Easter basket before. She knelt down to pat the Egg of Gold.

The animals were chattering very noisily when someone called in a loud voice:

"Make way for the EASTER RABBIT.

Here comes the EASTER RABBIT.

Make way! Make way!"

The crowd parted. In came White Rabbit riding in a flowery coach pulled by baby rabbits. In his arms he held a beautiful white lily in a pot. Round his neck was a wreath of violets and primroses and crocuses.

His face was covered with bright purple spots, but everyone was too polite to notice.

Only Old Graybeard the Goat, who didn't have any manners, kept saying under his breath:

"Freckle Face! Freckle Face!
Freckle Face for Easter!"

White Rabbit stood up and made a speech, and then gave the lily to Ann Eliza. He stepped backward gracefully—and stumbled over a baby rabbit. Down he went—a double somersault.

The animals tittered and cackled. Ann Eliza laughed, but White Rabbit didn't mind a bit.

He jumped right up again, made another bow, cleared his throat, and sang his song:

> *"Easter Rabbit, so they call me,*
> *Easter Rabbit fine and gay.*
> *Every spring I bring the children*
> *Easter eggs on Easter Day!"*

"Out of tune!" muttered Old Graybeard the Goat.

"Beautiful!" "Marvelous!" "What a voice!" "Clever Easter Rabbit!" cried the animals as they clapped long and loud.

"Happy Easter! Happy Easter!" Ann Eliza jumped up and cried, "A Happy Easter to you all! How can I ever thank you? But oh, how hungry you must be!"

So they all went to have breakfast in the Farmyard, where Ann Eliza gave them an extra round of grain and a head of lettuce apiece for a special Easter treat!